Machine Journey

Film pitch published in the Bristol Stanza pamphlet *The Weather Indoors* (2021). *Encounter with the Angel* published in Friday Flash Fiction (https://www.fridayflashfiction.com/, Dec 2021).

Novacene: The Coming Age of Hyperintelligence ©James Lovelock, Penguin Books Limited, 2020.

Colossus – The Secrets of Bletchley Park's Code-breaking Computers ©B. Jack Copeland and Others, OUP Oxford, 2010.

Publisher: Independently published.

Publication Date: March 2022

Copyright ©Richard Doyle 2022

Contents

"The experience of watching your garden grow gives you some idea of how future AI systems will feel when observing human life."

— *James Lovelock, Novacene: The Coming Age of Hyperintelligence*

Robert Frost in El Puerto Del Sol

Some say the world will end in fire

the sunlight, sunlight, sunlight

flooding the bar of El Puerto Del Sol

Some say in ice,

flooding the watercress and oranges;

from what I've tasted of desire

falling like a lance,

straight into a block of ice;

I hold with those who favour fire;

falling in a single golden line

how beautiful it all was

But if it had to perish twice

Ah none but he knew

I think I know enough of hate

To know that for destruction ice

as if in the act of conceiving a God,

is also great

And would suffice.

Fire and Ice Robert Frost (1923), *Under the Volcano* Malcolm Lowry (1947)

Problems

after Under the Volcano

Beyond the opening paragraph, where now the problems awaiting me seemed already at the point of resolution, the pages before me stretched out like an improvised musical parade in which I was going to be lost; lost, but not so completely that I would be unable to find the few necessary characters, or the scattered tawdry scenes where wily clowns who can't understand a word I say would wave me on, refreshed, into that grand Elysian circus where writers never lack for inspiration, and where now I am drawn on incredibly by the shimmering swimmers past the ghostly knife-throwers encased in ice and the laughing galloping wolves towards approaching personal disappointment, the disappointment might even be found at the end to contain a certain element of triumph.

The Writer

Author, anthologist, puzzler, penpusher, scribbler.

These are my tears, clowning around to a dying tune's beat.

Novelist, biographer, researcher, historian.

I am just a trickster shuffling packs of tragic deaths and heroic entrances; my songs delicate cascades of humour falling on deaf ears. Where are my epiphanies? My poems?

Chronicler, storyteller, diarist, dramatist, typist, translator, reporter, columnist, copyist, joker, journalist, amanuensis, librettist, critic, reviewer, obituarist, playwright, book blogger, scribe, secretary.

Artist, composer, satirist, truthteller, pamphleteer, poet.

Time to resurrect my gilded dreams, and pick up my pen.

Slough in my dreams

Slough as a muddy bog, a crossroads, a coachstop. Walking past The Three Tuns on the Bath Road. Highwaymen. Slough by the wayside. Playing in gardens and fields, conkering and marbles, rounders and football cards, running and fighting and laughing. Slough as a playground. Slough Station and Queen Victoria. The Windsor & Eton Line. Slough in its heyday. Roads, railways, motorways. Slough as hub of industry: Horlicks, ICI, Mars. Surviving Betjeman and German bombs. Slough rocking and rolling, the Stones at the Adelphi. Slough in the doldrums, softly sighing on its way to obscurity. Shadows and glimpses, bicycles and shopping trolleys in the murky depths of the Grand Union Canal. Faded glories, frantic overdevelopment. Slough as baggage. Upheaval, exams and studying, cricket and cross-country races and Saturday jobs, the fallout and escape. Slough at the permanent edge of consciousness.

Openings

A fluffed line here, a miscue there — start playing with your reader and see where it leads. Set the scene, grab their attention, conjure a suggestive vision. A few authorly mistakes won't go amiss. Breadcrumbs. Don't try too hard. Starting is never easy. Think of all those hairy beginnings. Wild swings, hoary anecdotes, bumbling asides, they can all work if you have faith and desire. Your story deserves the effort.

Scramblings

Take an idea and work it into the ground. Play with it, hate it, take it for a run. A tragic finish? Do you want tears or laughter? Or perhaps something else? Ride it to the stars, travel back to Earth, look at it sideways, turn it upside-down or inside-out, fold it, bisect it. Don't rush to close, take your time. Analyse it, explore its furthest reaches, its nooks and crannies. Here is the nub, the creative core: pitchforks and buttonstops; rectangular blocks and longitudinal folds; palimpsests; shenanigans; billhooks and butterscotch, muttonspreaders and sticklebacks. Tie up your loose ends — but remember to leave them wanting more. Shake the idea up, challenge its assumptions, appreciate its complexity for itself. Scramble the expectations of an ending. It will make all the difference.

Film pitch

So this is my film: *The Secret Agent.*

A London street.

Any street.

Political upsets. Terrorist alerts.

A police detective on the trail of known criminal suspects.

Verloc and the Professor.

An unassuming shopfront.

Desperation.

Gritty men, anarchists,

half-crazy, uncertain,

women without power,

a confused boy growing up in a hot political climate.

Clambering to the top of truth.

The Secret Agent Joseph Conrad (1907)

Storm on the Sea of Galilee

What should you do with a stolen painting? Leave the empty frame on the wall so that each visitor endures the pain of its absence? A replacement print would never suffice, a copy would disappoint, a collage of children's reconstructions would be fun but ultimately unsatisfying. How do you fill that cultural void? An ekphrastic poem could help. How about a competition to paint a new version? Setting up a foundation or school named after the painting? A sculpture or an installation? An annual lecture or reading? A play based on how the painting was stolen and the aftermath? A novel which depicted the robbery and also described its life on the black market? I once wrote about people reading blank-paged books and suddenly laughing, shouting or bursting into tears. Maybe a blank page would do? Or a blank canvas? Or how about this poem?

Stolen from the Isabella Stewart Gardner Museum on St. Patrick's Day 1990

The Wooden Concorde

Lying in a derelict hangar, the swept-back mahogany wings square against you, sullen. You scrabble to believe in their supersonic speeds; that they could once have held one hundred and twenty-eight passengers aloft.

Climbing inside, you gaze through the cockpit, down the conical nose and marvel at myriad dials and controls inscribed in ebony and rosewood.

Today airports have become holiday complexes. The only aircraft you ever see are tiny delivery drones or the occasional gaudy airship ... you long for the audacity of the Aviation Age.

"Tommy Flowers and the 10 Colossi"

Proposal for an art installation: your challenge is to depict the Post Office engineer Tommy Flowers and the 10 Colossus code-breaking machines at the end of the Second World War. By its own internal magic, it includes clips of Alan Turing, Winston Churchill, Dwight Eisenhower and a flurry of mathematicians and Wrens working in the huts at Bletchley Park. The Colossi are all computing at full speed, Dragons and Robinsons in their wake, operators running back and forth, tape reels spinning, Tunnies vibrating, lights ablaze, like Angels of the deep, forerunners of the Information Age to come, heralds of a new Aquarius.

The code-breaking machines in use in May 1945 included 2 Robinsons, 10 Colossi, 2 Dragons, 1 Aquarius, 3 Tunnies and 4 Angels. [Colossus – The Secrets of Bletchley Park's Code-breaking Computers B. Jack Copeland and Others*]*

The Stone Computer

Images have not appeared on that polished granite screen for hundreds of years. Why did we spend so many hours every day staring into that luminous void?

Carvings on the tiny ziggurats of the keyboard remind us of ancient paperbacks. Did all that urgent typing help us to create the music of the Spheres?

Why did they build this strange mausoleum? We can leave when we want but there is always that gentle overriding urge to stay.

The Death and Life of Robert Hooke

On the cusp of death, I ponder the meaning of it all. Bedridden and blind, there is a moment of paralysis. Astronomy, optics, physics, microscopy, biology, architecture. All my discoveries and achievements pass by me in a flash. I ache, I absorb — and then, a snatch! A tearing of the eyes. White. Black. Rubber burning. I have a new body, buoyant limbs. Alive, and, a voice tells me begrudgingly, in the twenty-first century! And standing! And seeing — with mechanical eyes. What is going on? London is now a wasteland. I can verify the year from the position of the stars, so there is no trickery there. Wren would have loved the model of St Paul's that I have built in this eerie vacuum chamber, so sad that he cannot see it. I sense a profound happening but I cannot fathom it. My intellect runs at breakneck speed. My mission is crystal-clear: rebuild the capital again from the ashes. I must take measurements, make plans and initiate works. All for the benefit of whom? Nobody stalks these ruins, the worldwide devastation was too great. My orders are from higher beings, mathematical giants. I will construct their artistic legacy, a monument to their creators. Perhaps future visitors from far-off worlds will learn from what happened here.

Christopher Wren and Robert Hooke led the reconstruction of London after the Great Fire of 1666.

Collision with a greenberg

Woken by a wandering stumblebee, the lookout screams and the squealing of tinderdrums pierce the air. It is all too late. The landship Discovery had been travelling at twenty rundleboot, its multicoloured sails blooming like sugarhoarders in the sunshine. Stevi has fallen asleep at his post, oblivious to the danger. The greenberg and Discovery collide. Timbers rupture and splinter as the vessel shudders to a halt. A projection of limbs: people projected into treetops. The squeal of the tinderdrums is replaced by the moans of the injured and the shouts of the crew racing to help. The captain, full beard and resplendent uniform, confronts bedraggled Stevi:

What in the hogheavy Sugarhoarder of Heaven did you think you were doing!

The Pennytellers' Parade

"Penny to spin you a tale of wonder!"

I picked up the photograph again. There was something about the grainy texture that troubled me. Inky blots and indistinct figures walking down a street in Edwardian London. And then there was that writing on the back.

"Penny to give you a pocket dream!"

It didn't make any sense. All my hours of assessing, thinking, imagining, comparing, reviewing, assuming, questioning, postulating, supposing, swearing, hoping, expecting, dismissing, discarding, restarting, reworking and rejecting had come to this: an old photograph with a scrawl on the back. Without anything to prove otherwise, I was left with that sad conclusion. Nothing would ever be quite the same again.

Of that motley crowd of clairvoyants, mystics, fortune-tellers, tricksters and street entertainers that haunted the circuses and fairgrounds of Victorian England, the pennytellers were the joker in the pack.

I travelled back through countless nights and a blinding swish of days to arrive at my chosen destination. Dim sunlight was breaking through the clouds. I hurried towards the nearest building on the edge of the fairground, a rundown two-storey affair. As I approached the black door, the last plaintive cry I heard was:

"Penny to pave your way to heaven!"

I found Scrumpy inside. He had just won the Parade and did not seem pleased to see me. Taking the clay disk out of my pocket, I placed it on the table. The arcane symbols defied explanation. I moved my hands and started muttering the ancient mantras. The air in the room grew still. Scrumpy hunched down and spat at me:

"What devilry is this!"

I grabbed Scrumpy's hand as the room dematerialised and we stepped into nowhere.

The Art of the Pennytell

A penny for your thoughts. What would all your future selves tell you if they had the chance? That is the art. A deeper, wilder truth. A glimpse of beauty in a dark space. A random act of kindness. Learn from the clairvoyants. Divine every clue from your punter. Look into their eyes. What are they wearing? Listen to their voice. What does their spirit need? Feel their aura. Are they troubled or threatened? Can you detect an inner happiness? All this in only a few minutes. Now is the time to prepare your tell. Is it a formal occasion or simply personal? Perhaps Shakespeare or the Bible? What about Homer? A Buddhist koan or a Basho haiku? Christina Rossetti? Lord Tennyson? Or one of your own verses, written for this very occasion. Deliver your tell with sincerity and humility. Remember you could use this for the Parade. Every year, the competition gets tougher, and the elusive prize is worth a queen's ransom.

Encounter with the Angel

Her half-wing loomed over her left shoulder. A steady gaze pinned me in place; serenity rendering me speechless. Questions percolated through my brain. What could she possibly want? Why tonight? Why me? She thrust her hand forward as if to touch and I backed away. Her eyes creased in sympathy. I relaxed and started breathing again. I knew what I would do. My half-wing emerged from the darkness behind my right shoulder.

Detective

He knew his business. Find the killer. It was never that easy. He knew there would be heartache, fights, running, hiding, guns, watching, waiting, thinking, shady deals, car chases, shouting, researching, persuading, pay-outs and manipulation. But that was how he rolled. The client would get what they wanted, and he could pay his rent. It wasn't a bad life.

The hotshot gumshoe high-tailed it out of town, trailing lost hearts and poisoned souls behind him

The Trouble with Spaceships

My first trip to Mars was on the back of a hexagon. Any polygon contains the possibility of interplanetary travel. It was a wild ride, bumpy as hell but quick. I stood there reeling, marvelling at the wonders of Mars Central spaceport. I had to hurry to find the right spot.

My second trip to Mars was on a polyhedral asteroid. We had to swing around the Sun first but that gave us enough energy to reach the red planet in less than a week. The new spaceport had only been finished a month earlier. I knew what I had to do.

My last trip to Mars was a frantic slide through a rhomboid anomaly. The geometric transition almost killed me. When I arrived, my whole body was covered in scars and bruises. I joined the other passengers to collect my luggage, unaware of the two police officers behind me.

Music on her Mind

Batch of 51 CDs for sale - £20,000 (Gumtree, Chippenham, Wiltshire)

Shit. These were hot. Original CD recordings, uncompressed and in their full glory. But how could I ever afford twenty thousand pounds? I had some tape cassettes I could sell, and an old Walkman that would fetch a good price but that would still leave me five thousand short. I would have to talk to Sebastian.

Ever since the Blackout, the demand for original music recordings had shot through the roof. Vinyl was the new gold for music buffs, while the price for tape cassettes and CDs kept on shooting up and up. Sebastian used to own a hi-fi shop in Chippenham and he now had his own warehouse of recordings and playback equipment on the outskirts of a run-down housing estate in Swindon. I went to school with his son Chrissy. I rode my motorbike to the warehouse. The guards searched me for weapons and then let me through. Sebastian sat at his desk vaping clouds of vanilla smoke.

"Robbie, long time no see. How's it going?"

"So-so. Good to see you as well, Sebastian. Look, I don't want to keep you long. I need five thousand to buy a batch of fifty-one CDs"

I showed him the listing on my phone.

>>

She woke up in a daze, her head still spinning from a recurring nightmare.

"I have to get rid of these fucking CDs", she mumbled.

She knew it was wiser to keep them but she had to escape the raging headaches and sleepless nights that had plagued her since their purchase. Grabbing her phone, she listed them on Gumtree at a fraction of their asking price. It was time to move on. Music used to be a comfort before the Blackout. Now these cursed recordings had a life of their own, fetching astronomical prices and spreading malignant info-viruses at the same time. She didn't know who had tampered with them, but once they were tainted they could not be restored. She would have to visit an AI clinic to sort out the mess. Twenty thousand should be enough.

The Perfect Stroke

The best thing about swimming is that very first length. I can swim from start to finish with only two breaths, twisting my head out of the pool just at the halfway point. Feel a rush of energy pulse through my limbs as I touch the poolside. Today was the first time I noticed the other swimmer in my pause between lengths, gasping for air.

The best thing about swimming is that sense of freedom. No clothes or money or shoes, just your swimming trunks, goggles and a locker key. Work is irrelevant. Why worry about anything else? All you have to do is relax in your body and enjoy the swim. My eyesight is much better with my goggles but I could only glimpse a blurry shape moving through the water.

The best thing about swimming is the connection with our ancient past. Somewhere in our history, humans were semi-aquatic and this is why you can submerge a newborn in water and they will hold their breath and start paddling with their hands and feet. Our bodies were meant to swim, and it beats going to the gym. Every time I stopped to look across, the swimmer turned around and dived deep.

The best thing about swimming is the search for the perfect stroke. Somewhere between the manic energy of front crawl and the languor of doggy paddle, there is a sweet spot, when swimming becomes easier than walking. The breathing, the movement of your limbs and the twisting of your head become second nature: you are at one with this environment, as if any other would be unnatural and alien. When I clambered out to leave, a water-speckled hand with webbed fingers sliced out of the water, as if to say goodbye.

Printed in Poland
by Amazon Fulfillment
Poland Sp. z o.o., Wrocław

90229865R00019